Ninja Pug 3

All-Out Attack

Amma Lee

INTRODUCTION

Jiro and Luna are back in the third installment of the Ninja Dogs series in "All-Out Attack," where they plan to put an end to Monukuma's dubious ploys. This time, they will have the help of Ryoichi, Hanzo's grandson, who wants to make amends for everything that he's done under Monukuma's mind control. After taking several weeks off from tracking down and defeating Monukuma, Jiro, Luna, and Ryoichi find themselves in a time-crunch. After going back to the hotel where Monukuma hurt Hanzo, Jiro, Luna, and Ryoichi learns that there is one more culprit in on Monukuma's plan. Our three heroes will face obstacle after obstacle, but Jiro, the ninja pug leader, will keep Luna and Ryoichi on their toes. In "All-Out Attack" will Jiro, Luna, and Ryoichi put an end to Monukuma's plan of world domination, or will they be dominated by Monukuma's power?

CHAPTER ONE

Jiro looked in on Hanzo and sighed once he realized that Hanzo was sleeping. It had been a few weeks since Hanzo was discharged from the hospital, but the old man was still having a hard time returning back to his usual self. Hanzo often walked around like he was in pain, but he tried to put a brave face on for Jiro, most importantly, Hanzo sought to put a brave face on for Ryoichi.

"Ryoichi," Jiro murmured, as he thought about the young teenage boy who was asleep in the next room. Three months ago, thieves had broken into Hanzo's and Jiro's home and stole some valuable books. Jiro and Luna, the white-haired poodle, tracked down the culprits. To both Jiro's and Luna's surprise, the culprits were ninjas, and one of them resembled Hanzo's long lost grandson, Ryoichi. Jiro knew then that he wasn't going to rest well until he found out the truth!

A few weeks after the fight between Jiro, Luna, and the thieves, Jiro and Luna learned of the ninjas' plans to hurt the president! Jiro and Luna were not going to let that happen. They tracked down the ninjas and learned of the ninjas' real plans, and Jiro confirmed that the young ninja that he had fought before was in fact Ryoichi. Things only got crazier after that.

Hanzo had been guarding the president for weeks because he knew that the president may be attacked. Jiro and Luna learned that Hanzo and the ninja clan's leader, Monukuma, were once friends. Ryoichi had regained his memories, and Hanzo was hurt in an intense battle with Monukuma. Jiro, Luna, and Hanzo were able to successfully save the president from being harmed, but things weren't over yet. Monukuma was still on the run with the ninjas that he'd brainwashed.

"We must figure out something quick before Monukuma tries to do more damage," Jiro said to himself. They managed to take back Hanzo's missing books, which could have helped the ninjas slowly destroy the world, but Jiro was sure that Monukuma and his clan still had much more up their sleeves.

Hanzo had started sleeping in more and training less since his injury, so Jiro knew he'd have to train harder for the both of them. While the humans slept, Jiro would train. He might even visit Luna to see if she was relaxing under the stars. The two of them needed to talk about their next steps. When Jiro left Hanzo's bedroom, he almost let out a small yelp when he saw Ryoichi standing right outside the door. Jiro couldn't sense Ryoichi at all.

"I thought I sensed you in here," Ryoichi whispered. Jiro started thinking that Ryoichi's ability to hide his presence from others, including animals, was improving. "The old man.... I mean... grandfather is alright, right?" Jiro nodded his head quickly because responding to Ryoichi would have been pointless. Ryoichi could understand some of Jiro's actions, but at the end of the day, Ryoichi could not speak "dog."

Jiro looked at Ryoichi and grinned showing sharp teeth. Even though Hanzo wasn't at his best right now, Jiro was glad that the old man had received at least one of his family members back. *No wonder the police couldn't locate Ryoichi though*, Jiro thought to himself. If Ryoichi was taken in by powerful ninjas and brainwashed, the police stood no chance at finding the then ,very young Ryoichi.

"You're about to go train, aren't you?" Ryoichi asked. After Ryoichi regained his memories and started to live with Jiro and Hanzo, Ryoichi had been watching Jiro intently. Jiro was a bit uncomfortable at first because he was starting to think that maybe Ryoichi would turn on him and Hanzo, but Jiro immediately destroyed that thought. Ryoichi was impressed with Jiro's ninja abilities. Ryoichi even told the small pug that he felt odd learning from a dog, but Ryoichi believed Jiro to be a real ninja, unlike Monukuma.

Jiro looked at the young boy, and Ryoichi gave him a warm smile. Nodding his head, Jiro turned on his paws and made his way downstairs. Ryoichi followed earnestly behind him. Jiro thought that it was nice to have a training buddy. Jiro was glad that Luna often trained with him, but Jiro got most of his training done at night, and Luna wasn't always up when he was training. Though Jiro thought the teenage ninja needed his rest, he'd never turned down the opportunity of teaching Ryoichi his ways.

"Ryoichi, I'm going to show you the ninja ways of a real honest ninja, and not of a criminal.

****

"You're up early," Jiro said as he walked through his yard over to Luna's. The white poodle was on the porch watching the birds play in a small puddle.

"Yes, I had a feeling you'd come over today with instructions," Luna said, keeping her eyes fastened on the birds. To be honest, Luna had come outside every morning since the incident at the hotel waiting for Jiro to tell her their next moves. Luna was surprised that it had taken Jiro this long to reach out to her. Almost as if reading Luna's thoughts, Jiro voiced his opinion on that very subject.

"Luna, sorry for not reaching out to you sooner," Jiro said sincerely. "I've had a lot on my plate with

Ryoichi and Hanzo. Hanzo's not one hundred percent yet, and Ryoichi has been studying under me as my disciple. He really feels bad about what he's done and what happened to Hanzo. I needed to give him extra attention to try to tell him that what happened wasn't his fault." Luna nodded her head. Jiro didn't need to explain anything to her because she already knew.

"Jiro, I understand. No need to explain. If everything's cooled off, we need to do something about Monukuma and those brainwashed ninjas!" Monukuma and his crew were getting out of hand. First, they broke into Jiro's and Hanzo's home, then they went after the president and injured him. Whatever those pesky humans were planning next was more than likely going to be more dangerous.

"You're right," Jiro said nodding his head. They need to find Monukuma and his clan again and see what they were planning to do next. They still didn't know the full story behind what Monukuma was planning, so they needed to get some insight into that. Ryoichi would more than likely play a significant role in that.
Jiro sat down and looked at the sky as he thought about everything that needed to be done to put an end to Monukuma and his devious ploys.

"We need to go back to that hotel and track them," Jiro said. Going back to the ninjas' headquarters to find that Monukuma and his crew were at the hotel worked, so he didn't see why them going back to the hotel wouldn't work.

"I agree, but it's been a few weeks since they've been gone," Luna said this last time, but this time she had more to add. "I think they would have taken more drastic means to erase their scent from us. They might have thought that we were slightly skilled dogs before, but I'm sure that this time they see us more of a threat." Jiro growled when Luna mentioned that possibility. Still, there wasn't anything else that they could possibly do. Even if they did figure out another way, Monukuma might have already made his move.

"I know, but this is the only lead we have right now. We've been sitting behind the scene not doing anything at all. Yes, that was my fault, but now we kind of have to hurry things up." Luna could see that Jiro was tormented by their loss of time. It was true that they weren't actively pursuing the ninjas in the past few weeks, but Jiro wasn't fully one to blame. It was Luna's fault too for not pushing him, but the pug needed time to handle his business.

"Jiro, please don't blame yourself, this isn't entirely on your shoulders. You and I are doing a lot for the world. We both needed to take a break and we deserve a break. If we worked continuously, we would be burned out and then who would save the world? Some humans? No, we're the right dogs for the job." Jiro grinned at that. When Luna was serious and encouraging, she really knew what to say to make Jiro feel better.

"We're a great team, huh?" Jiro asked, and Luna returned his grin.

"Of course! We'd be nothing without each other."

Jiro and Luna had a lot on their plate now as they were moving forward to put an end to Monukuma and his ninja clan. However, they knew that they would be able to do anything Jiro and Luna put their mind to, as long as they believed in each other.

Jiro could feel in the pit of his stomach, that the end of this horror show that Monukuma was trying to put on would reach its finale soon.

CHAPTER TWO

"It'll be easier to jump through the trees," Ryoichi said, as he followed closely behind Jiro and Luna as they made their way to the hotel. There were a lot of people on the street, and the dogs kept tripping people as they ran through their legs.

"The boy's right, but there aren't too many trees close together," Luna said to Jiro. Jiro looked up and made a mental note of the distance between the trees. It'll be a far jump, but if Ryoichi was sure that he could do it, then Jiro and Luna should be able to do it as well. Turning around while maintaining his speed, Jiro nodded to Ryoichi. The boy smiled and jumped as high as he could. Following Ryoichi's lead, Jiro and Luna jumped into a nearby tree as well.

"I'm not entirely sure where Monukuma and the others are heading, but with your dog senses, I'm certain that we'll be able to track them," Ryoichi said as Jiro, Luna, and Ryoichi jumped from tree to tree with precision.

"Easier said than done," Luna responded and shook her head in agitation. She hoped that the ninjas' scent would still be lingering around the hotel. Luna was almost confident that the hotel staff would have done a complete sweep of the place once they were permitted to return to the hotel. The hotel staff might have thrown out or given important information to the police. Jiro wasn't too keen on stealing information about the ninjas from the police. They'd never understand that they were trying to help.

"Luna, we have to stay positive. We will be able to find Monukuma by tracking his scent at the hotel. It'll be more difficult, but we can do it!" Jiro knew that the odds appeared to be against them, but that didn't mean anything. Jiro did his best work when his back was up against the wall.

"The hotel's just up ahead," Ryoichi said as he jumped down from the last of the trees in their reach. The next tree wasn't for another mile, and none of the three ninjas had that type of skill to jump that far. "I probably won't be able to get too close to the hotel. I wasn't wearing my face mask when we infiltrated the place. The staff might recognize me and call the police." Ryoichi said sadly.

Ryoichi was a good kid, he had just been misled. Even if Ryoichi explained that to the cops, they'd never believe him. There wasn't a doubt in Jiro's and Luna's mind that Ryoichi's face was caught on cameras. There was no way Ryoichi was getting out of the hotel without having to commit more crimes. It was best that Ryoichi hid.

The three of them stopped running then and looked around. There weren't a lot of people walking around the hotel because of the fear of what happened a few weeks ago with the president being injured. People were definitely uneasy around the large hotel.

"I'm going to go ahead and see if I can see how many people are in there," Luna said, leaving Jiro and Ryoichi alone. Jiro turned towards Ryoichi and looked at him. Jiro needed to convey his message in a way that Ryoichi would be able to understand him. It was unfortunate that Ryoichi wasn't able to speak to animals like that young girl from that one cartoon show, so Jiro needed to think quick. Looking towards the ground, Jiro found his answer. Dirt! Jiro could write his message in the dirt with his paw. Jiro wagged his tail happily and started writing his message in the dirt.

We won't be long. Keep an eye out for anything suspicious and whistle loudly if you see or sense danger. Luna and I will come out running. And remember, we are in this together.

Ryoichi read Jiro's message and smiled.

"You're right, we're in this together. Thank you for

believing in me. Let's stop Monukuma's plans and save the brainwashed ninjas and the world.

****

It didn't take Jiro and Luna too long to stealthily search for clues in the hotel. There weren't a lot of people in the hotel and Jiro was thankful for this, but he did feel bad for the humans who owned the hotel. They were more than likely losing profit. Even though Jiro and Luna didn't come across any opportunities to get discovered, they also didn't find any clues related to Monukuma and his clan.

"What now?" Luna asked. "My nose isn't picking up any of those ninjas. I was right in thinking we waited too long to do this." Jiro frowned at that. Jiro hated that Luna was so pessimistic, but the poodle was right. Their noses weren't able to pick up anything on the ninjas.

"Please tell the president that we are truly sorry that he was attacked at our hotel!" Jiro and Luna heard a voice, and they quickly ran over towards a dark curtain and hid between them. They looked through the small opening and was surprised to see the vice president walking with, what seemed to be, the manager of the hotel.

"Humph... the president will have a lot to say about the security of this hotel when he's well." the vice president said scornfully. "Be gone, I need to make a private call, and your cameras better be off!" the vice president said. The manager of the hotel bowed to him and quickly exited the room that they were in. Jiro and Luna were so quiet at that moment that they barely breathed.

The vice president looked around making sure that nobody was around and pulled out his telephone. After tapping his feet on the floor tile angrily, he finally started speaking again.

"This hotel was the perfect spot for you to do the job!" Jiro and Luna listened to the vice president's conversation intently. What exactly was he talking about? "There is no way that your people should have failed…. What? What's that you say? Two dogs and an old man? I don't care! The hospital stated that he will be perfectly fine, meaning that you failed!" The vice president was so angry that he was shaking. "We had a deal… I gave you my complete cooperation, told you confidential information. All you needed to do was to seal the deal. Get rid of him, and when the world was in a frenzy, you take over it by a storm. I was supposed to get one of the highest positions in the New World!"

"Jiro, are you hearing this?" Luna asked as her eyes grew wider. Jiro nodded his head with his mouth hanging open in shock. They went to the hotel for clues related to the ninjas' whereabouts, and just when they were sure that they failed, this happened.

"This…. this sounds a lot like the vice president and

those ninjas are working together," Jiro said. Jiro didn't want to make an assumption like that, but that's what it sounded like.

"We need to meet to think about how to approach this. The police are snooping around, and I don't want anything to link this to me. Where are you?" The vice president paused for a minute. "The Razzle's place? That's in the middle of the forest. Nobody goes there anymore. There's a lot of fungi and mold there. That building is completely uninhabitable…. Well… no one would think to look for me there. Some of your people are hiding out at my villa here, I'll have them escort me there. See you soon, Monukuma." The vice president looked around again and made a speedy retreat.

Jiro and Luna emerged from behind the curtain and grinned at each other. The information that they just overheard was exactly the information that they needed.

"Let's get back to Ryoichi. We have an evil plan to stop," with that said, Jiro and Luna made their way to an opened window.

CHAPTER THREE

"The vice president? I don't think anyone in our organization knew that we were working together with the vice president." When Jiro wrote out everything he and Luna had heard in the hotel, Ryoichi was at a loss for words. He wasn't aware of this, and nobody else had mentioned that they were working together with the vice president. Why was that kept a secret from everyone in the organization? "Maybe only Monukuma and Ootori knew about it?"

"Jiro, do you think it's possible that Monukuma is misleading everyone in the organization? I don't see any reason to keep that information from them unless he's planning something behind their backs." Jiro sat down and began scratching his ear as he thought. The fact that the vice president helped the ninjas attack the president was surprising enough. Jiro sighed.

"I'm truly at a loss here. As soon as we find out something important, more things are introduced.

Where do we even begin?" Jiro asked. No matter how confusing and shocking this newfound information is, Jiro, Luna, and Ryoichi will figure out a way to solve it.

"Hey, guys… I can tell you're talking in your little dog language, but I can't help if you don't let me know what's going on," Ryoichi said. Jiro and Luna looked at Ryoichi and nodded their heads in understanding. It didn't take Jiro long to write out everything that had transpired between the two dogs. Ryoichi read what Jiro had to say and started rubbing his chin.

"Jiro, are we going to pursue Monukuma and the vice president today? We've spent a lot of time in the hotel, and this time I think we should have a solid plan before jumping into this mission." Luna suggested. Jiro was the type of dog who ran head first into danger without a plan in mind. Jiro preferred planning on the go; however, Luna didn't think that was a good plan this time.

"No, we need to follow the vice president to Razzle's Place. I know what you're thinking Luna. I know you believe we need to come up with a good plan of attack to handle this situation, but it's too late now. It's either now or never. If we let the vice president meet with Monukuma, there's no telling what would happen." Jiro knew that he was saying everything that Luna didn't want to hear, but facts were facts.

"Whatever you say, Jiro," Luna said and sighed. "You're the boss. Take the lead, and I'll follow you." Luna thought that they should be cautious, but as usual, they were heading head first into a dangerous situation.

"Razzle's Place is about 45 minutes by car. If we stick to the trees and run as fast as possible, we might be able to beat the vice president there." Ryoichi suggested. "You two are dogs and have incredible senses, but we're going to a rundown unkempt forest and knowing Monukuma, he will try to hide his scent from everyone. Our best bet is to try to beat the vice president there and follow him."

"Not a bad idea," Luna said nodded her head in agreement. Luna thought the boy was intelligent for his age, but she would have never guessed that the kid was this bright. "He's a smart kid," Luna said looking at Jiro and Jiro grinned proudly.

"Just like his grandfather," Jiro said.

The three of them moved quickly through the trees as they ran like their lives depended on it. In a sense, their lives did depend on it. If they failed at stopping Monukuma, his crew, and the vice president, there was no telling what tragedies will fall upon the world. Plus, if they failed, Hanzo would be in trouble too and Jiro would never forgive himself if more horrible things happened to Hanzo. Jiro, Luna, and Ryoichi will make sure that he and the rest of the world were protected.

After what felt like an eternity, Jiro, Luna, and Ryoichi had arrived at their destination.

****

"Ugh… this place makes my head hurt," Luna complained as she inhaled the scent of the forest. It smelled horrible! "Why would someone build something in the middle of this place?"

"Judging by your face and reactions," Ryoichi began, "you're probably wondering why a building is in the middle of this forest." Luna was impressed by how observant the young boy was. "This forest wasn't always like this. The family that used to live out here were kind of weird, but they took care of the forest. When they left, it was almost as if they took the forest's soul with them."

"I see," Jiro said, but he honestly didn't understand how a forest so grand only flourished when humans were around. Jiro always believed that humans were the blame for when plant and animal life started decaying. At any rate, an environmental science lesson wasn't the reason that they were there. Ryoichi grinned then like he had read Jiro's thoughts.

"We can talk more about that later. We need to keep our eyes and ears peeled. I don't sense that the vice president has arrived yet." Jiro was happy that the young ninja was taking the initiative. Jiro was proud that the boy was able to learn proper ninja skills versus skills to harm. Luna, on the other hand, was thankful that Ryoichi was cautious, unlike their pug leader.

"Better be careful, Jiro," Luna said playfully. "If you don't be careful, young Ryoichi here will surpass you and become our leader." Jiro wasn't an arrogant dog, so he wasn't going to say that it'll take years for Ryoichi to surpass him. Jiro was actually looking forward to the day that Ryoichi surpassed him. Jiro believed since Hanzo had no family left, that Jiro would have to be Hanzo's successor. Now that Ryoichi was back in the picture, Jiro no longer needed to be the heir. Ryoichi was the rightful heir, and Jiro and Hanzo would train him until he's ready.

"I'm looking forward to that day. I can see it in his eyes that he's a natural born leader." Jiro complimented the boy. Ryoichi shifted from side to side uncomfortable, and Jiro knew right away that it was because Jiro and Luna were talking and weren't letting Ryoichi in on the conversation.

When Jiro was about to carve his compliments into the tree branch, his ears perked up at the sound of a car approaching. Looking towards the direction of the sound, Jiro's eyes widened as he saw a long car approaching with blacked out windows. Jiro believed that those large cars were called "limousines." Jumping down to some branches towards the bottom of the tree, Jiro focused his ears and eyes on the car. When the car stopped, the vice president jumped out.

"Look, I don't want to be in this place at all! You two better get me in there and out without any of that disgusting filth touching my clothes!" the vice president brushed out the wrinkles in his suit jacket. Jiro looked towards the two ninjas that accompanied the vice president and recognized them right away as being Ootori and Ryoichi's friend, Zen.

"What is Zen doing here?" Ryoichi asked perplexed. "He's never told me anything about the organization working with the vice president. We're best friends! Well at least…we were best friends." Since regaining his memory, Ryoichi hasn't seen the boy. Ryoichi was also sure that Monukuma told the slightly older boy lies to make Zen not want to be friends with Ryoichi anymore. They needed to save Zen from his brainwashed state, they needed to save everyone who had been brainwashed.

Jiro looked up at Ryoichi and saw the pain in the young ninja's eyes and immediately knew what the boy was thinking. Placing his paw on Ryoichi's hand, Jiro comforted him. Ryoichi must have had mixed emotions about seeing his former teammate and about having to possibly battle him. This Zen kid was special to Ryoichi like Hanzo was special to Jiro. When they're finished handling the vice president and Monukuma, they would help the kids that had been brainwashed. Jiro knew that they would succeed because when he put his mind to doing something, he got it done.

CHAPTER FOUR

Jiro, Luna, and Ryoichi managed to maneuver quietly through the trees as they followed behind the vice president, Ootori, and Zen. After Ryoichi briefly showed Jiro and Luna how to partially hide their scent, Jiro and Luna mastered it and was able to follow behind the culprits with ease. Ryoichi was impressed and also ashamed. It took him three years to learn how to partially hide his scent, yet it took two dogs moments to find out how to fully master it! These dogs were truly something else.

"Zen is a little bit more advanced than I am," Ryoichi whispered, not taking his eyes off of the trees in front of them. "He may be able to sense me, but I believe the rotten smell of the forest will hide my scent." Both Jiro and Luna nodded in agreement. They also believed that the putrid smell would give them an advantage of tracking them without detection.

"How long will this take? It smells horrible in here!" The vice president complained.

"A few more minutes, sir," Ootori said with a cool and calm voice. "This would go by so much quicker if you allow me or Zen to carry you."

"Bah! I don't want either of your DNA on me!" The vice president shouted. "If for some reason Monukuma's backup plan doesn't go smoothly, I don't want anything linking me to your organization!" It was clear that the vice president and Monukuma were a part of some conspiracy to conspire against the president and the world, but Jiro wasn't sure what kind of conspiracy they were dealing with.

"We understand your need to feel secured," Ootori chuckled. "We're faced with a minor obstacle. Monukuma-sensei will have the solution!" Jiro frowned at this. Ootori was so sure that Monukuma would be able to pull off what they're planning, but Jiro thought otherwise. Ootori saw Jiro's and Luna's strength, plus Monukuma trained Ryoichi. The man was clearly underestimating Jiro and his group.

"They're convinced that we won't be a problem," Jiro said. "I wonder why that is? We've ruined their plans twice, I would think that they'd be warier of us." Ryoichi looked over at Jiro and guessed what the dog was talking about.

"It's because Grandpa is at the hospital," Ryoichi suggested. "I think Monukuma thinks you and Luna were attacking the organization on Grandpa's orders. I believe he looks at you two as being highly trained dogs like police dogs. He probably doesn't think you understand humans in our entirety." Luna looked over at Ryoichi and then looked at Jiro.

"That's a plausible point. With Hanzo in the state that he's in, there's no way he'd order us to attack Monukuma because he wouldn't be able to provide backup. I think we should use this to our advantage versus being upset that he's underestimating us," Luna suggested and Jiro thought that was an excellent suggestion, but then Jiro thought of something else.

"Hanzo clearly said when he came to the hotel and saw you and me there that he was surprised to see us there. I don't think Monukuma would forget that." Luna sighed. All this thinking about the way humans think was making her head hurt.

"He might have forgotten, he might not have heard, who knows how human brains work!" Jiro wasn't convinced by Luna's response. There was definitely something fishy going on here, but Jiro didn't have enough information to go by.

"I'm sure you two are having a great conversation," Ryoichi said as his jumps from tree to tree slowed. "but we're here. They couldn't sense us, but Monukuma is stronger than the three of them. We can't just be talking, or in your case quietly barking, because he might hear." Jiro and Luna nodded their heads and came to a complete stop once they approached a run-down building. The vice president, Ootori, and Zen knocked on the door several times before the door opened.

"It took you long enough," there was no way that Jiro could forget the voice of the human who had hurt Hanzo. It was Monukuma! This time Jiro could feel in his bones that this cat and mouse game was going to come to an end.

****

"We need to get inside," Jiro whispered once the door to the building closed. Even though they did not have a set plan of action, they could at least say that they weren't planning to just wait outside while Monukuma, Ootori, Zen, and the vice president had their meeting. Jiro looked at Ryoichi and nodded his head towards the building silently asking what the best way to get in there without detection was.

"We've been to this hideout once before, so I don't know the layout entirely," Ryoichi answered Jiro's silent question. "As far as I am aware there is only one entrance. There's no windows or anything, and there shouldn't be any cracks small enough for us to enter despite how rugged it is. We have no choice but to use the front door." Ryoichi said and shrugged his shoulders.

"Well... that's not the best option," Luna murmured. She wished the boy had told them that earlier, but it wasn't like the situation would have been any different. Luna doubted that new entryways would have been made for them if they had known in advance.

"That's definitely not ideal, but I don't think they would be having their meeting close to the door. It's a pretty big building, I'm sure Monukuma and the rest of them are somewhere else." Jiro said, trying to help Luna stay positive. Jiro didn't think this mission was going to be easy, so he wasn't surprised when Ryoichi told them they had no options when it came to entering the building.

"I'm ready when you two are, but please remember even though we're more than likely walking into battle, we should avoid harming the vice president." Luna looked at Ryoichi as if he had two heads.

"Jiro, is this boy crazy?" Luna asked in surprise. "The vice president is plotting something terrible! He's an enemy!" Jiro shook his head.

"Yes, he's an enemy of the world; however, he is still the vice president. If we were to harm him, we are no better than those ninjas who hurt the president." Luna frowned but said nothing else to this. Jiro looked at Ryoichi and nodded. Ryoichi grinned and got in a stealth position. Jiro, Luna, and Ryoichi approached the door quickly and silently. Ryoichi pressed his ear to the cold metal door and listened. He didn't hear anything beyond the door.

"I don't think they're in the room directly beyond the door," Ryoichi said and tried turning the knob. He wasn't surprised to find the door locked. Reaching into his back pocket, Ryoichi pulled out some lock picking tools. Jiro couldn't help the grin that spread across his face. Ryoichi sure did come prepared.

"Ha! I knew you foolish dogs would come here," Jiro, Luna, and Ryoichi froze at the sound of the voice. Ryoichi turned quickly and was face to face with his former best friend, Zen. "I didn't think you'd join these dogs' cause. You've changed Ryoichi, so I'm not going to hold back. I will take you down not only as instructions from Monukuma-sensei, but for me the person you betrayed!"

Jiro, Luna, and Ryoichi didn't have enough time to react before Zen made his attack.

"Ah!"

CHAPTER FIVE

"Ah!" Ryoichi cried out when he jumped out of the way of Zen's powerful front kick. If that had connected with the young ninja, Ryoichi wouldn't have been able to help Jiro and Luna.

"Tsk... fast as ever I see. It's no matter though, you three are not interfering with the organization's goals any longer!" Zen said and teleported away from Ryoichi's quick punch.

"Luna! We must help Ryoichi. If Monukuma or Ootori come and investigate the commotion, we'll lose our edge on them!" Jiro said, and Luna nodded her head in agreement. Both Jiro and Luna got into a fighting stance.

"There's no time for all of us to focus on Zen," Ryoichi called out as he made every effort to dodge Zen's attack. The other teen was slightly stronger than him, but Ryoichi had picked up a thing or two after training with Jiro the past few weeks. There was no way he was going to allow Zen to overpower him.

"Jiro, what should we do?" Luna asked. The door was locked and plus it was metal. Even they weren't powerful enough to break down such a heavy door. Almost as if Ryoichi could understand Luna's thoughts, he threw his lock picking tools over to Jiro.

"Use this! With your quick learning abilities, I'm sure you'll be able to take care of the door. Don't worry about me, I'll take care of Zen. You two stop Monukuma, Ootori, and the vice president!" Ryoichi turned back towards his opponent and made attacks of his own.

"Heh, I'll finish you off quickly and take care of those mutts," Zen said, as he dodged attacks left and right from Ryoichi. Jiro was worried about the young ninja, but if Ryoichi believed that he could take care of Zen, Jiro and Luna would leave the other young ninja to him.

"Luna, we got to make this quick!" Jiro said. The tools that Ryoichi gave them looked like they required fingers and thumbs, but Jiro was going to make the object work for him no matter what. Placing the lock pick between his sharp teeth, he stuck it into the door.

"This has to work, this is our only option!" Luna repeated to herself. She watched the pug as he attempted to open the door with the tools and watched the battle between Ryoichi and Zen. What was there for her to do? Ryoichi didn't want them to waste their time with a fight that is between two friends, and Jiro was busy with trying to get the door open. She was the only one not contributing.

Jiro noticed Luna's unease and stopped what he was doing.

"Luna, find something hard to push into the lock pick! I get how this is supposed to open the door, but I need more force to push it deeper into the door."

"Right, be right back," Luna said and ran off. It didn't take her long to find what she was looking for. Between her small mouth was a brick. "When I get close to you move away quickly so I can throw it into the lock pick!" Luna mumbled. It was hard for her to form coherent words with a brick in her mouth. Jiro nodded his head and waited for Luna to get close enough. Once she was close, she threw the brick hard into the lock pick.

Click!

The door made an audible clicking noise, and with a hard push of Jiro nose, the door was wide open.

"Tsk!" Zen sighed when he noticed that the dogs opened the door. Ryoichi noticed Zen looking away and did a roundhouse kick knocking Zen down. "Ah!" Zen called out in pain.

"Keep your eyes on your target, Zen!" Ryoichi yelled and turned towards his comrades. "Good luck!" Jiro and Luna nodded and ran through the door. When they got inside, they were expecting to take a two-second breather, but that would have been too good to be true. Entering the building, they were greeted by Monukuma, Ootori, and the vice president!

****

"Well... well... well," Monukuma said, grinning from ear to ear. "Looks like I've underestimated you two, but no matter. Soon you two will be like old man Hanzo. Tell me, is he up and running yet?" Monukuma said, and Jiro growled in anger. How dare he disrespect Hanzo!

"How did these dogs get in here?" the vice president asked, confused. Ootori shook his head.

"Mr. Vice President, that doesn't matter right now," Ootori turned towards Monukuma then. "Sensei, I will take him to a more secured location with the new plans. The kids should be in the chambers being reeducated with your mind control device. I'll turn it off and send them your way." Monukuma shook his head then.

"No, this time I'm going to fight them. These dogs need to learn who their true master is," Jiro narrowed his eyes and quickly moved them over to

Luna. Luna was ready to attack, she was just awaiting orders from Jiro. The conversation that they were currently having was meaningless to Jiro right now. "Take him and go!" Monukuma said, and Ootori grinned.

"Yes," with a blink of an eye, Ootori and the vice president disappeared.

"Luna! Chase after them! Don't let them get away!" Jiro called out, and Luna frowned in confusion.

"What about him? He's strong, and I can help you!" Luna knew that she always made it seem like everything that she did was such a bother, but she wasn't the type of poodle to turn her back on a friend.

"I'll take care of this," Jiro said confidently. "We cannot let the vice president and Ootori get away. We need to take all three of these humans down. Please Luna, stop Ootori and the vice president," Luna closed her eyes as she contemplated everything. Luna knew that Jiro was right. This time they couldn't let any of these humans go. Justice will be served.

"Okay, but take care of yourself!" Luna said and made a run out the door. Jiro briefly looked towards Luna's retreating back and smiled. *We got this*, Jiro thought to himself.

"You told your little friend to leave? That was very

foolish of you," Monukuma chuckled. "You two might have bested my students and stolen my star student from me, but you're overly confident. You are dogs and I am a man, there's no comparison." Jiro growled again heated. Monukuma knew exactly what to say to get under the little pug's skin.

"You three won't get away with this," Jiro said though he knew the older human wouldn't be able to understand him. "I'm going to...no... we're going to stop you no matter what motive you have!" Monukuma didn't know what Jiro had said, but when he noticed the little pug get into a fighting position, Monukuma knew that the time for talking had come to an end.

"Little doggy, I'm going to show you how real ninjas fight," Monukuma said seriously this time. A few seconds passed, and neither one of them said anything. After a while, their two bodies crashed into each other.

CHAPTER SIX

"Ugh!" Jiro groaned as his small body was pushed back against the wall. Jiro understood then that Monukuma was going to go all out on him. Jiro blinked one second and the next second Monukuma was in his face preparing another blow. It took all of Jiro's power to block Monukuma's powerful attack.

"So, what do you think about my full power, dog? It's nothing like my students'!" Jiro bared his teeth and went in for a strike of his own. Jumping high into the air, Jiro focused his power and mimicked Monukuma's teleporting move. Jiro appeared behind Monukuma and just when he thought he had the advantage, Monukuma turned around, and backhand slapped him away.

"Ah!" Jiro said as he flew backward. Catching his balance in the air, Jiro brought one of his paws down and did a back flip so that he could land on all fours. *Jiro, this isn't the time to falter! He's not impossible to defeat*! Jiro thought to himself. Jiro attacked Monukuma, but none of his moves were connecting. Did he really overestimate his own power?

"You're no match, dog," Monukuma said chuckling. To Monukuma, he was already the champion. "Once I take care of you and that other dog, I'll take Ryoichi back. If he doesn't cooperate, he'll be destroyed as well. This world belongs to me. Ever since I was starting off as a young ninja, I knew that I could not live in a world where I had to follow someone else's rules." Because Monukuma believed he would ultimately win this fight, Monukuma thought he might as well tell the dog what he was planning.

Jiro listened on as Monukuma spoke without stopping his attacks.

"I want this world to grovel at my feet. So I brainwashed an army of young ninjas to join me in my cause. They believe that they will be on equal footing with me, but that's not the case. Their heads are filled with lies, I only need them to do my bidding. There's no point in getting my hands dirty when I can have others doing it."

"So... you were just using them?" Jiro asked, knowing full well that Monukuma wouldn't understand him.

"One day I saw the vice president jogging in the park, so I kidnapped him to brainwash him and have him as a spy. Unfortunately, my plan didn't work, but fortunately, the vice president was intrigued by my idea. As long as I make him a high-ranking member of the New World, he'd help me with funding. We were going to turn this world upside down, but I needed the right moves to help me with defeating anyone who stood in my path."

"So that's why you stole Hanzo's Hakumoto books?" Jiro's and Luna's journey to stop Monukuma and his organization started from Monukuma having Ryoichi and Zen break into Hanzo's and Jiro's home.

"It would have gone as I planned if it wasn't for you two dogs and Hanzo! We were to destroy the president, make it seem like another country did it, and while everyone was confused, that's where I would have come in a taken this world by a storm! I'll make you pay for interfering with my grand plans. You all will pay!"

Jiro closed his eyes and thought of his dear friend Hanzo. The older man was probably at home in bed in pain because of this evil man. There wasn't a doubt in Jiro's mind that Monukuma was stronger, but there was no way Jiro was going to let Monukuma win. He would protect Luna, Ryoichi, the brainwashed ninjas, the world, and most importantly, Jiro would protect Hanzo.

"You're mine!" Monukuma shouted as he made a dash towards Jiro. Jiro cleared everything from his mind except the willpower to defeat Monukuma.

Jiro stood on his hind legs and moved his paws slowly in a circle. When Monukuma was close enough to Jiro to the point that he could feel Monukuma's aura, Jiro opened his eyes and jumped towards Monukuma with a powerful punch.

"Ugh!" Monukuma shouted in pain as Jiro's paw connected with his face. Monukuma flew backward into the wall, breaking through it and landing on his back in the next room. Jiro didn't even have to get up and look. Closing his eyes, the small pug knew that he had won.

****

"How's the old man?" Luna asked when she saw Jiro making his way over to her yard.

"He's fully recovered. Hanzo and Ryoichi are out making up for lost time." It's been a few weeks since Jiro defeated Monukuma, but he still remembered that day like it was yesterday. Jiro's powerful punch had knocked Monukuma out cold, and when he was sure that Monukuma wouldn't be getting up anytime soon, he had made his way outside to check on his comrades. Jiro wasn't surprised to see that Ryoichi had defeated Zen and had a good grip on both Zen and Ootori.

Ootori was no match for the white poodle and gave up when he saw how well Luna fought. Ootori was more of the advisor to the group. He knew the ways of the ninja, but Luna knew the ways better.

Frightened by what would be done to him by Jiro and his group, Ootori was the one who called the police and confessed to what they were doing.

When the police got there, they were surprised to find the vice president, but it didn't take much explaining from Ryoichi and Ootori to see the evil ways of the vice president. The police took the unconscious Monukuma, Ootori, Zen, and the vice president into custody. After freeing all the young ninjas from their mind control, they released Zen. Ryoichi and Zen made up and were back to being best friends.

"So, I guess we got our happy ending?" Luna said looking over at Jiro. Jiro grinned and nodded his head. The last few months had been crazy, but he wouldn't trade the experience for the world. Even though they no longer had to worry about Monukuma; Jiro, Luna, and Ryoichi agreed to still help people in need. They were going to start their own ninja organization to help people, not to destroy people.

"Yup, we got our happy ending," Jiro said peacefully. Jiro laid down on the porch on his back and looked at the sunny blue sky and smiled. He was glad that Hanzo had Ryoichi now and he was happy that Hanzo was happy. Everything had worked out perfectly well. Luna mirrored Jiro's position and looked towards the sky as well.

Neither one of them would have ever imagined that they'd be put into the situations that they were put into. They've learned many things about each other which helped them become a great team. Even though they had overcome a grand ordeal, they knew that their job was to continue to protect the people of the world and the people that they cared for.

Jiro smiled as a thought entered his mind. If they were ever presented with a similar situation in the future, they would give it they're all in an all-out attack because that was their ninja way.

The End

CHARLIE
BOOK

Made in the USA
Middletown, DE
13 August 2017